Good Night, My Dear Child

By Joanna Roth

Illustrated by Stephanie St. Denis

Tellwell Talent
www.tellwell.ca

ISBN
978-0-2288-0163-4 (Hardcover)
978-0-2288-0164-1 (Paperback)

Dedication

I dedicate this book to the ones who inspire me every day. To my loving, supportive husband Darcy, I thank you for everything you do for me and our family! And, to my dear sweet little souls Lexi, Mya and Kayson, I thank you with all my heart for giving me this tremendous opportunity in being your mother. You truly have inspired me to share these words.

Good night, my dear child.
The day is now through.
Time to get cozy and calm.
Time for a deep breath or two.

Our day was busy.
We laughed, played and cried.
We danced, sang, ran and jumped.
We may have even lied.

We do many things
for no rhyme or reason.
I love all the things we do
as we go through the seasons.

SPRING

SUMMER

FALL

WINTER

In the cool spring breeze,
we plant peas, beans and corn.
We might see worms in the dirt
or some bees beside us swarm.

We can pet our kittens
and throw a stick for our dogs.
We can watch the geese fly by
or sight some leaping frogs.

In the hot summer,
we can play at the beach.
We may fish in the evening
and prepare a big camp feast!

In the frosty fall,
we may jump in the leaves.
We can feel our first season frost
and listen to the swaying trees.

In the brisk winter,
we can skate across the ice.
Perhaps, we go snowmobiling
and fall more than twice!

Moments may not be perfect
but I want you to know,
you are the light of my life.
You make my heart always glow.

So now my dear child,
let's give thanks for this day.
Let's count all our blessings
and close our eyes and pray.

Good night, my dear child.
I loved our day together.
I'll always love you the MOST!
To the moon and back,
always and forever!

About The Author

Born and raised in the small town of Hafford, Saskatchewan, Joanna Roth lives on a farm with her husband and three dear children. They try to live a fairly simple life and enjoy being around home. Reading to her children before bed is one of her favourite times as a mother, which inspired her to write this book. So, get cozy and quiet and enjoy these short and sweet words with your little ones!

CPSIA information can be obtained
at www.ICGtesting.com
Printed in the USA
LVHW071917020719
623039LV00004B/19/P

9 780228 801641